# The **Mystery** of **UFOs**

# The Mystery

# of UFOs

by
Judith Herbst

illustrated by
Greg Clarke

ATHENEUM BOOKS FOR YOUNG READERS

For Summer, Jack, Mr. Bix, and June Bug
–G. C.

Atheneum Books for Young Readers
An imprint of Simon & Schuster Children's Publishing Division
1230 Avenue of the Americas
New York, New York 10020
Text copyright © 1997 by Judith Herbst
Illustrations copyright © 1997 by Greg Clarke
All rights reserved including the right of reproduction in whole or in part in any form.
Book design by Angela Carlino
The text of this book is set in Frutiger Bold.
The illustrations are rendered in watercolor, india ink, and gouache.
First Edition
Printed in Hong Kong by South China Printing Co. (1988) Ltd.
10  9  8  7  6  5  4  3  2  1
Library of Congress Cataloging-in-Publication Data
Herbst, Judith.
The mystery of UFOs / by Judith Herbst ; illustrated by
Greg Clarke.—1st ed.
p.   cm.
Summary: Relates the stories of a number of famous UFO sightings, including the purported crash
of an alien spaceship in Roswell, New Mexico, in 1947.
ISBN 0-689-31652-6
1. Unidentified flying objects—Juvenile literature.
[1. Unidentified flying objects.] I. Clarke, Gregory, ill. II. Title.
TL789.2.H47   1997
001.9'42—dc20
95-45845

This is Route 375 in Nevada. It is long and lonely
and tantalizingly flat, the perfect place to land a UFO.
Four big signs along the highway invite any aliens who
may be in the area to set their ship down here. It is
the only official landing strip for flying saucers.
Greetings, extraterrestrials. Welcome to Earth.

The Yakima people of Washington State have a very curious legend. Long, long ago, they say, a man with red eyes came to live with the tribe. He was wise and had great powers of healing, and when he grew old, he said, "Soon I will die. You must take me now to a special place I will tell you about."

The people did as the red-eyed man had asked. When they saw that he was comfortable, they left him to make peace with the spirits. ✳

Night fell and a cool wind blew gently across the land. The silence deepened. The red-eyed man's chest rose once and then was still. Death had come for him. And a few days later, something else came for him.

According to the legend, an object descended from the sky to claim the body of the red-eyed man. What it was the Yakimas cannot say, but the legend lives on. It is a tale to tell when the night is full of stars.

Something awfully strange seems to be going on. People—lots of people—insist they are seeing things in the sky, things that nobody can identify. These things, say the witnesses, are balls of light, ovals and disks, metallic shapes that appear and disappear, almost like magic. They reportedly land in wheat fields and meadows and occasionally leave behind scorch marks and patches of flattened grass. They have been seen drifting over houses while shocked witnesses scramble for their cameras. They hover above highways, humming softly, or blasting the pavement with blue-white flames. Car radios go dead. Engines stall. Headlights flicker and fail. And then the thing—whatever it is—moves on, sliding back into the silence of the night.

They have come to be called UFOs—unidentified flying objects—and apparently people have been seeing them for thousands of years. In biblical times they were called glowing disks and giant wheels. Native Americans told about flying canoes. Woodcuts and paintings from the 1500s show strange cylinders and arrows filling the sky. In the 1800s, the UFOs were cigar-shaped "cloudships," and today, they are saucers, flying saucers. And we still don't know what they are.

What has come to be known as the first sighting of a "flying saucer" was probably just a mistake. It happened on the afternoon of June 24, 1947. Businessman Kenneth Arnold was flying his private plane over the Cascade Mountains in Washington State. Suddenly, he spotted a flash of light outside the plane. He looked out and saw nine objects flying in a V-formation against the distant peaks of Mount Baker.

At first, Arnold thought they were jets because they were moving so fast. But when he worked out their speed, he began to have serious doubts. The "jets" seemed to be traveling at an amazing seventeen hundred miles an hour—more than twice the speed of sound! Were they some kind of experimental aircraft?

Arnold stopped briefly at Yakima, Washington, and then continued on to Oregon. But the reporters had already gotten word of the strange sighting. They were waiting for Arnold when he landed.

"Mr. Arnold, exactly what did you see?" they asked.

Arnold struggled to find the right words. At last he said, "They flew like a saucer would if you skipped it across the water." And that's all the press needed to hear. The flying saucers had officially arrived. Or had they?

UFO investigator Dr. J. Allen Hynek later showed that Arnold had guessed wrong about the objects' distance. If they'd been as far away as Arnold thought, they'd have to have been tremendous or Arnold wouldn't have been able to see them at all. So that meant they were going much slower than seventeen hundred miles an hour. What, then, did Arnold see? Most likely, said Hynek, it was a flock of birds. And as for flying saucers, that's what the press had called them. All Arnold had said was that he'd seen something flying—and indeed he had.

But less than two weeks later, something was in the skies over New Mexico, and it certainly wasn't birds.

On July 1, 1947, an unknown object showed up on three different radar screens. It was moving very fast and making what seemed to be impossible maneuvers. Nobody had any idea what it was.

The following evening, Mr. and Mrs. Dan Wilmont of Roswell, New Mexico, saw a metallic object pass over their house. They said the object looked like two saucers set rim to rim.

Friday, July 4. During a severe thunderstorm near Corona, ninety miles northwest of Roswell, rancher Mac Brazel heard a thunderclap that didn't sound like the others. Moments later, two other people saw something fall out of the sky toward the direction of Roswell. Surprised radar operators watched as the unidentified object they had been tracking suddenly disappeared from their screens. They assumed it had crashed.

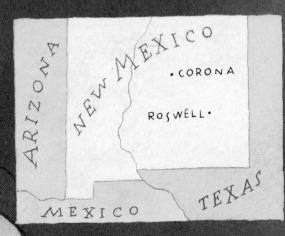

The next morning, two people who had been camping north of Roswell discovered the crash site. They were the first ones on the scene. Then came a sheepherder and a group of archeology students. They all described the same thing. What they saw, they said, was some kind of spacecraft. It was shaped like a delta wing. It had crashed into the side of a slope and had been ripped open. And there on the ground, in the shadow of the wreckage, were three or four small bodies. Their arms and legs were thin. Their eyes were widely spaced. Their heads were large and hairless. And no, the witnesses agreed, they did not look human.

At the same time, Mac Brazel had come across a lot of strange debris on his ranch. Some of it looked like tinfoil, he said, but no matter how hard he tried, it wouldn't crumple. It just straightened right out again, good as new.

Brazel also found support beams that hardly weighed anything at all. A few of the pieces were marked with what Brazel described as "hieroglyphics of some sort."

On July 6, Brazel drove down to Roswell and reported his find to the sheriff, who notified the nearby army base. Almost immediately, the side roads near Roswell off Interstate 285 were blocked off, and air intelligence officer Jesse Marcel was sent to investigate. Within twenty-four hours, the military moved in and swept up every bit of crash debris on Brazel's ranch.

The next day, the "bodies" that had been found a few miles away were reportedly shipped out to Andrews Air Force Base in Washington, D.C. The military then issued an official statement: The object that crashed outside of Roswell, New Mexico, was a weather balloon.

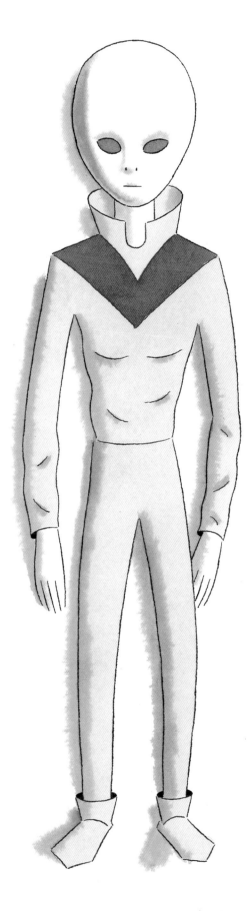

But despite what they said—or didn't say—about the crash in New Mexico that weekend, the air force was starting to feel uncomfortable. Unknown objects were showing up on radar. Mysterious balls of light were seen flying over top secret areas and missile test sites. More and more people were insisting they had seen UFOs. And a year after the Roswell incident, air force pilot Thomas Mantell died while chasing something he couldn't identify.

Mantell never really got a good look at the object, which is why it is considered unidentified. It was always above him, and he had to keep climbing to stay with it. It was tremendous, he said, and metallic. Mantell was at an altitude of 22,000 feet when he radioed the base that he was going higher to try to close in on it. A short time later he lost consciousness from lack of oxygen, and his plane crashed.

The official report from the government said that Mantell had been chasing the planet Venus. But it doesn't seem likely that an experienced pilot would fail to recognize the brightest and most familiar planet in the sky. It's easier to believe that Mantell had been fooled by a giant Skyhook weather balloon. The Skyhooks were made of a silvery material and could climb to tremendous heights. Since the Skyhook project was secret, Mantell probably didn't know about it. Also, if the government suspected that Mantell's unknown object was a Skyhook, they weren't about to admit it.

But the air force was still worried. More and more pilots were reporting encounters with strange lights which seemed to "follow" their planes. So in the 1940s, the air force set up Project Sign to investigate the problem of UFOs. As the sighting reports poured in, they were studied by a team of scientists. And amazingly, Project Sign concluded that UFOs could actually be extraterrestrial spacecraft! But this did not suit the air force one bit, and Project Sign was immediately shut down.

Next came Project Grudge in 1948, but it was a halfhearted effort. Captain Edward Ruppelt, who headed up the project, thought the whole "UFO thing" was just a big pain in the neck. But little by little, Ruppelt began to have second thoughts. By the time the air force changed the name of Project Grudge to Project Blue Book in 1952, Ruppelt had truly become interested in solving the UFO mystery. However, there were far more sighting reports than the Blue Book staff could ever investigate, and most received little, if any, attention.

As a result, a dissatisfied public decided to take matters into its own hands, and private UFO research groups began to spring up. In Blue Book's final report, the air force officially declared that most UFOs are either planets, optical illusions, hoaxes, meteors, or weather balloons, and in 1969 they closed their files.

PROJECT
BLUEBOOK
PROJECT
GRUDGE SIGN

# WHAT UFOs ARE NOT

BALL LIGHTNING

LENTICULAR CLOUDS
(LENS-SHAPED)

SUN PILLA

FLYING PANCAKE
(NAVY EXPERIMENTAL CRAFT)

METEOR

VENUS

BLIMP LIGHTS

But it was certainly not an optical illusion that flew over Paul Trent's farm in McMinnville, Oregon, in May of 1950. Trent's wife was the first to spot it. She was in the backyard feeding rabbits when she caught sight of the disk. As it glided silently toward her through the cloudy skies, she shouted for her husband to bring out a camera. He was able to get two photographs before the object disappeared.

The McMinnville photographs have been studied by a number of experts. Recently, they were analyzed by a computer. And the results are very interesting indeed.

It seems the Trents really did photograph a solid object. It measured about one hundred feet across and was more than half a mile away when the pictures were taken. There is no trace of support wires or strings. In other words, it was big; it was three-dimensional; and nearly fifty years later, it remains unidentified.

One of the most famous unsolved cases is the so-called Socorro UFO. On April 24, 1964, a local policeman, Lonnie Zamora, came across an egg-shaped craft moments after it landed off Route 85 in Socorro, New Mexico. Zamora had been chasing a speeder when he heard a roar and saw a blinding blue flame low in the southwest. Worried about fire, Zamora gave up the chase and went to investigate.

The craft was at the bottom of a ravine. It was whitish in color and sat on four long legs like some huge metallic insect. The door to the craft was open, and Zamora could see a narrow ladder that reached to the ground. Two beings in white coveralls were outside the craft. They were about the size of young boys, Zamora said. They didn't look especially alien, just small.

Zamora wondered if maybe he was seeing something he shouldn't see, like an experimental space vehicle. Socorro is not very far from the White Sands Missile Test Range. But just as Zamora leaned into his car to use the radio, he heard an earsplitting roar. He whirled around in time to see the craft lift off on a column of blue flame. Seconds later it was gone.

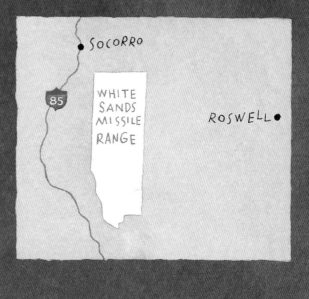

When investigators went to the scene they found physical evidence that something had most definitely been there. There were four clear impressions in the ground that seemed to correspond to the four landing pods Zamora claimed to have seen. Also, bits of metal were discovered clinging to a rock close to one of the impressions. Could a landing pod have scraped against it as the craft touched down? Most revealing was the depth of the impressions. Measurements showed that whatever made them had to have weighed at least eight tons.

So the question here is not whether Lonnie Zamora saw a craft of some kind touch down and then take off. The question is: Whose craft was it—ours or theirs?

In 1957, there had been a flurry of UFO sightings in and around Levelland, Texas. Levelland is about forty miles east of the New Mexico border (see map). Almost all the witnesses had reported seeing the same glowing, egg-shaped object that Zamora would describe seven years later. Some said it had touched down, blocking the road ahead of them and causing their car engine to fail.

It should be noted, however, that 1957 marked the beginning of the "space race." In October, the Russians sent up Sputnik, the world's first artificial satellite. For a number of years, American and Russian scientists had been working furiously to put something into space. So you have to wonder what kind of secret vehicle testing was going on at White Sands at the time. Did Lonnie Zamora and the people in Levelland see the secret test flights of an experimental craft, or did they really encounter a spaceship from another planet?

NEW MEXICO

ROSWELL

· LEVELLAND

TEXAS

MEXICO

Most astronomers believe that there is life elsewhere in the universe, but they doubt we are being visited. The biggest problem, they say, has to do with distance.

Stars are separated by trillions and trillions of miles. Even if we could build a super-fast spaceship, it would still take hundreds of years to reach just one or two of the closest stars. And nobody knows if any of these stars have planets, let alone intelligent life. So for us at least, it makes more sense to send radio signals instead of sending ourselves. If another civilization picks up our signals and beams back a message, we can make contact without leaving home.

But maybe the aliens aren't anything like us. Maybe their life spans are much longer than ours, so big trips don't bother them. Or maybe they've discovered shortcuts. They might know a way to fold space or just punch right through it. That could explain how UFOs seem to appear and disappear and change direction so quickly. Take, for example, the object that played cat and mouse with an air force bomber in 1957.

It was early morning on July 17. The RB-47 bomber was on its way back to Forbes Air Force Base in Kansas. Sometime around 4:00 A.M. the radar operator picked up a blip on the radar screen. Something was approaching the aircraft from the right side, and it was moving mighty fast.

A few minutes later, a blinding bluish-white light appeared from out of nowhere and shot straight toward the plane. The pilot and co-pilot were so shocked, they couldn't even react. The light closed in and then, all of a sudden, changed course and vanished. But half an hour later it was back, "as big as a barn," said the pilot, just below the nose of the bomber. The crew was beginning to sweat.

UFO

The mysterious light stayed with the bomber for almost two hours. It darted this way and that, zigzagging across the sky. The crew watched in amazement as the light seemed to stop dead in its tracks before shooting off at a very high speed. Then, just as the plane was nearing Oklahoma City, the light winked out and was gone.

Scientists tell us that a real spacecraft couldn't possibly do any of those things. The stresses caused by sudden starts and stops and ultra-sharp turns would break the ship apart. So are UFOs solid objects or aren't they? If we are to believe the eyewitness reports, sometimes it's hard to tell!

MANEUVERS

Many years ago, the famous psychiatrist Carl Jung (pronounced YUNG) became fascinated by the subject of UFOs. He didn't necessarily think they were spaceships, but he believed that people were seeing something real.

Jung wondered if people could be creating UFOs themselves. The UFO, he said, would start out as a picture in our minds, like the images we create when we dream or hallucinate. But in this case, thousands of people would be imagining the same picture: a flying saucer.

Jung didn't think it mattered that not everybody had been to the movies or seen drawings of flying saucers. They didn't even have to know what a flying saucer was. The important thing, said Jung, is that everybody knows the shape. The circle or disk is a common symbol in all cultures.

Jung knew that the mind can be very powerful. So what would happen, he asked, if a hundred thousand or a million minds all imagined the same shape? Could that shape somehow become a solid object? And if it could, it might explain how UFOs can be real and not real at the same time.

But there is one more piece to the UFO puzzle, and no one quite knows where it fits. Over the years, thousands of people have insisted they were kidnapped by strange beings and taken aboard UFOs. The more ridiculous stories are probably not true. But psychiatrists and UFO researchers who have interviewed some of the victims feel that most of these people are describing a real experience. The question is: What kind of experience was it?

The stories are surprisingly similar. Sometimes the person comes across a landed UFO on a lonely road and is taken aboard. But more commonly, he or she is awakened in the middle of the night to find small, alien-looking creatures standing by the bed. The victims all say they couldn't move and believe the creatures had somehow paralyzed them. They were then "floated" out of bed, through the wall, and up into a waiting UFO.

After a painful and frightening medical exam, the victims are returned home. They rarely remember what happened and are surprised to find bruises or little puncture marks on their bodies. They often learn the full story through hypnosis.

But couldn't this all be just a powerful hallucination? Psychiatrists say maybe, but they wonder why so many people would have almost the same hallucination. So far, the nature of these "alien kidnappings" remains a mystery.

We have come to the end of the book, but we have not solved the mystery of UFOs. The researchers continue their work. They investigate sightings and interview witnesses. They pore over landing sites, carefully searching for even the tiniest piece of evidence that something real has been there. They study the photographs that come in, the ones that show metal disks, and strange balls of light, and dark, shadowy shapes.

Reports of UFOs continue to fly. Perhaps they are spaceships from other galaxies. Perhaps they are wondrous visions from our own minds.

Perhaps one day we will know.

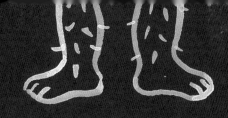